If You Give a Mouse a Brownie

If You Give

a Mouse a Brownie

WRITTEN BY **Laura Numeroff**

ILLUSTRATED BY **Felicia Bond**

Balzer + Bray
An Imprint of HarperCollins *Publishers*

For Donna and Alessandra—
with love and appreciation
—L.N.

ISBN 978-0-06-027571-6 (trade bdg.) — ISBN 978-0-06-027572-3 (lib. bdg.)

16 17 18 19 20 PC 10 9 8 7 6 5 4 3 2 1
❖
First Edition

If you give a mouse a brownie,

he's going to ask for some ice cream to go with it.

When you give him the ice cream,

he'll ask you for a spoon.

He'll start drumming on the table.

Drumming will get him so excited he'll want to start a band.

You'll have to play guitar.

He'll want to put on a show,

so you'll have to build a stage.

Then you'll need
some spotlights and
a microphone.

When the stage is finished,

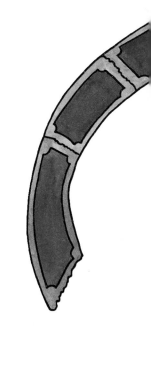

he'll want to make lots of tickets.
You'll have to find paper and markers.

When the tickets are done,
he'll decide to make posters as well.

He'll hang them all over the neighborhood.

When he's out hanging them, it might start to rain.

He'll fold some posters and make a little boat.

Then he'll sail it in a puddle.

He'll get so wet he'll start to sneeze.

You'll have to put him in your pocket to stay nice and warm.

When he peeks out of your pocket, he'll smell something delicious. The smell will remind him that he's hungry.

You'll have to take him to the store
and get a few things to nibble on.

Of course, he'll want to have a picnic.

When the sun comes out, you'll have to take him to the park. While you're setting up the picnic, he'll see a playground. He'll jump on the swings.

He'll go as high as he can.
When he looks up at the sky,
he might notice a big white cloud.

The cloud will remind him of ice cream.

He'll probably ask you for some.

And chances are,

if you give him some ice cream,

he'll want a brownie to go with it.